I Hate Projects!

Written by
Susan F. Tierno

Illustrated by
Jessica Schiffman

Senior Editor
Michael McGuffee

Think-kids®

To Ed Carola, who hates projects!
– S.F.T.

For my daughter, Jamie, with love from Jessica
– J.S.

Think-kids® is a registered trademark
of Creative Thinkers, Inc.

Published
by
Creative Thinkers, Inc.
8 South Street
Southfield Suite #10
Danbury, CT 06810
1-800-841-2883

ISBN 1-58237-017-6
ISBN 1-58237-000-1 (20-book collection)
Library of Congress 98-071347

Printed in the USA.

I hate projects!

I can never decide what theme to
study. I asked my mom what to do.

She said, "Oh, that's easy. Pick a theme that is most interesting."

5

But I still couldn't decide.
So I asked my big brother.

He said, "Oh, that's easy. Pick the
one that's easiest to do."

But I still couldn't decide. So I asked the principal.

She said, "Oh, that's easy. Pick the one
that you don't know anything about."

But I still couldn't decide. So I
asked the librarian.

She said, "Oh, that's easy. Pick the one that has the most information."

11

But I still couldn't decide. So I asked my teacher.

He said, "Oh, that's easy.

You pick the one you would

learn the most from."

I Hate Projects!

Think-kids® think about it...

Projects need plans,
ideas, and a theme.
Projects require plenty
of thinking time.